When Pigs Can Fly!

by Carol Madou

Illustrations by Dan Drewes and Justin Reilly

AuthorHouse™
1663 Liberty Drive
Bloomington, IN 47403
www.authorhouse.com
Phone: 1-800-839-8640

First published by AuthorHouse 3/21/2011

ISBN: 978-1-4567-3534-0 (sc)

Library of Congress Control Number: 2011901430

Printed in the United States of America

authorHOUSE®

I thank my husband John and son Edward for their encouragement,
and enduring the long process of my finished book.

I also recognize my mom and my co-workers for all of their support.
(including Debbie, whom I'm looking forward to meeting soon)

A special thanks to Megan and Justin for helping to bring my story to life.

- Chapter One -

IT'S SPRING!

The cold weather of winter finally disappeared! Warm sunshine returned, with colourful buds on the trees and birds with their happy songs. They promised the start of a bright new season. Some new baby animals arrived on the farm too. Spring was here! Eddy's favourite time of year! It was like magic with all of the excitement and wonder.

Eddy felt like the luckiest boy in the whole world. For the nine year old, every day was filled with many adventures on his family's farm. Several kinds of animals lived on the farm, so the young boy had many companions. Each one was special and unique. There were wooly lambs, furry rabbits, and feathered chickens. Day after day, Eddy spent hours with the animals and watched them grow.

Spring was the best time of year on the farm! There was excitement with new baby ducklings, rabbits, and litters of pigs.

They were all tiny, soft, and cute. When the young rabbits were a few weeks old, they looked like balls of fur and were a perfect size for cuddling.

When Eddy arrived home from school, he quickly changed into his farm clothes. He was in a hurry! But there was a hug for his mom, before he left the house. The nine year old ran as fast as his little legs would go, along the narrow path to the barns. But he slowed down and waved to his dad before he entered any of the barns. Today, the excited farm boy went straight to the barn where the young piglets lived. When the newest litter of baby pigs arrived, Eddy quickly picked a favourite from the group. Because of his small size, Eddy chose the name Peanut for this piglet. This piglet was tiny and one of a kind!

Inside the barn, Eddy was very worried when he couldn't find his special piglet anywhere. Nervously, he ran all around the barn and looked for Peanut. Eddy was scared! Then suddenly his search was over! The young piglet was finally found in the large pen near the back door of the barn. Eddy almost cried when he saw the small animal huddled up in a corner, all alone. He gently lifted Peanut, and moved him back with the other piglets.

"Stay here and be warm Peanut. My dad put these lamps here for you and the other baby pigs."

This gentle animal was very important to Eddy. He loved the tiny piglet, and wanted to keep him safe. But the young farm boy was puzzled. He couldn't understand why his favourite piglet was always separated from the other pigs. Eddy did not want Peanut to be alone!

Before Eddy left the barn, he made sure that Peanut was near the other piglets and under the lamps. With his piglet safe and sound, he walked quickly to the next barn to visit the friendly and fluffy rabbits. These soft furry animals were fun to hold.

- Chapter Two -

WHO IS PEANUT?

Eddy was extra quiet at school all week. He was worried about Peanut. On every visit to the barn, he found his favoured piglet alone in the same corner. Each time, he tenderly moved the young animal back under the lamps.

On Friday afternoon, Eddy came home from school at his usual time and dropped his backpack onto the front hallway bench. But when he ran out the door, he still wore his school clothes. His dad was busy with the ducks, and didn't notice his son's outfit. Eddy still waved, and went straight to the pig's barn. He wondered where he would find Peanut this time.

That was hours ago. It was dinnertime, but Eddy had not returned to the house. His mother wasn't too worried though, because she knew that he was with some of the farm animals. But she didn't know which group of animals or what barn. By chance, Eddy ran onto the front porch, just as his mother walked outside.

"You're late today! Where have you been Eddy? Your dinner is ready and on the table." They walked into the house together.

"Sorry mom. I had to take care of Peanut," Eddy answered.

In the kitchen, Eddy saw his dad waiting for them.

"Who is Peanut?" his mother asked.

"He's my favourite baby pig. Dad called him the lop-eared piglet when he was born."

"Yes, I remember him, with his long ears," Farmer John replied. "I've never seen such long ears on a young pig before."

"It makes me sad when Peanut is all by himself. I stayed longer with him today instead of visiting the other animals. Every day Peanut is far away from the other pigs. I always find him alone."

"I'm glad you're taking special care of Peanut. It's the weekend, so you can spend more time with him tomorrow."

"You're supposed to change into your farm clothes before playing in the barns, Eddy. Go wash up quickly, and join us at the kitchen table", his mother instructed. The family ate their dinner and soon it was bedtime for Eddy.

Eddy went to find Peanut the next morning, but did not see him with the other piglets. After searching the barn, he found Peanut in the outside pen. Again, the small animal sat alone in the far corner. He wondered why this young piglet was always by himself!

9

- Chapter Three -

LEAVING THE FARM!?

A few days later, Eddy got a surprise after school. Dressed in his farm clothes, he quickly walked into the kitchen. But then he suddenly stopped. He stood completely still and stared across the room. He couldn't believe his eyes. Grandpa came to see him! His visit on a school day was completely unexpected.

Eddy ran across the kitchen floor towards the tall bearded man, and received a giant hug.

"Grandpa!" Eddy called out with excitement.

"There's my Eddy!"

"You surprised me!"

"Your mom and dad invited me over for a visit."

"I'm glad!" Eddy stretched his arms out for another hug. Instead, he was lifted up into the air. The boy's soft cheek rubbed against his grandpa's beard, and a huge smile appeared on his young face.

Eddy looked over at his mom and dad after Grandpa put him back down onto the floor. His parents looked sad. He was confused.

"We're happy that Grandpa is staying with us for a few days," his mom said.

"You don't look very happy."

"We have something to tell you Eddy," his dad said in a serious tone of voice.

Eddy glanced up at Grandpa with a worried look. He walked slowly over to his kitchen chair and sat down. His dad told him the bad news.

Suddenly, Eddy was on his feet. He didn't want to hear anymore! Before his dad finished speaking, Eddy ran out of the house.

Eddy only heard a few words about how his family might have to move away from the farm. He understood now why his parents looked so sad. No matter what, he never wanted to leave the farm and all of the animals! His dad's announcement made him very upset and unhappy. Eddy was shocked by the news, and he didn't stay to hear the reason for leaving the farm.

- CHAPTER FOUR -

A FLYING PIG!

Eddy ran as fast as possible towards the barns. Feeling very sad, he needed to be with his favourite young piglet. When he found his pet, Eddy hugged him tightly. He didn't want to lose him! A few minutes later, as he held Peanut, his Grandpa stood in the barn and saw him crying.

"Grandpa, you have to talk to dad. We can't move and leave Peanut! He's my best friend!"

"Is this Peanut you're holding?"

"Yes it is! He's my favourite, and I picked him on the day he was born."

"He's small, but those ears are amazing!"

"Dad called him the lop-eared piglet."

"That's a good name, and so is Peanut."

"I'm worried Grandpa."

Eddy told his Grandpa how the other pigs always left Peanut on his own.

"That reminds me of another pig that lived on this farm when I was a boy. I named that young pig Windham, because I think he wanted to fly."

"Tell me Grandpa!"

Eddy continued to hold Peanut as he sat down on an old wooden bench near the animals. Grandpa sat beside him and looked down at the young piglet. With Peanut on his lap, Eddy moved closer to his grandfather. When all three of them were comfortable, Grandpa started his story.

"I was nine years old, I think," Grandpa said.

"Same as me!"

"Just like you, I visited the animals every day. Then one day, I got a surprise when I walked into the pig's barn. All of the pigs were in the barn, but they stood together in a group. It was very unusual. The pig I named Windham was in front of the other pigs. Windham jumped up and down, and looked like he was trying to fly. A flying pig! Isn't that funny?"

"They don't have wings Grandpa!"

"No they don't. But there's a well-known saying about flying pigs."

"Tell me Grandpa!"

"It will only happen when pigs can fly. Someday, you'll understand Eddy. But Windham's odd movements made me wonder if he was telling a joke to the other pigs."

"Do animals talk to each other Grandpa?"

"I think they do. I've seen some evidence right here on our farm."

He paused, and smiled at the puzzled look on Eddy's face.

"I stood by the barn door and watched the group of animals. When Windham stopped jumping, it sounded like he was laughing! I've never heard a pig make such a noise before. All of a sudden the strange noise stopped, and Windham looked around at the other pigs. None of them moved. It was so quiet. The only sound in the barn was the crackling noise from the straw."

"His joke wasn't funny?"

"Windham lowered his head and stared down at the ground. He looked very sad. Windham had tried to fit in with the other pigs. They were all the same color and liked to play in the mud, but these pigs were not his friends."

"Why do pigs play in the mud Grandpa?"

"The mud helps to cool them and to keep insects away. Pigs are actually very clean animals, and can get sunburned."

"I'll keep Peanut out of the sun! What did you do next Grandpa?"

- Chapter Five -

TALKING ANIMALS

"I moved away from the barn door, before the pigs noticed me," Grandpa continued.

"Did you see Windham again?"

"I watched him walk slowly out of the barn. He was all by himself. Suddenly, I heard some loud and unfamiliar noises that came from another part of the farm. An odd honking sound was very noticeable. It was different than the clucking noises made by the hens and ducks on the farm. In fact, it sounded like the animals were fighting. There was a thunderous sound of splashing water, which was also strange and puzzling. That part of the farm was usually quiet."

"Windham must have heard the commotion too. He suddenly stopped and looked around in all directions."

"Curious about the noise, I headed towards the grassy area where the small stream flows through our farm. Windham followed me down the path. He walked as quickly as his short legs would carry him. When we arrived, there were several groups of farm animals standing on both sides of the water."

"What were the animals doing Grandpa?"

"Along with all of their noise, there was a lot of activity with wings flapping, and tails swinging. The animals weren't fighting, but with their necks stretched out, it looked like they were talking to each other! I could only imagine what they were saying."

"Where did it come from?" Grandpa asked as he pretended to be a duck.

"I don't know," Eddy answered in his best duck voice.

"Looks different from us," Grandpa said as he tried to cluck like an old hen.

"Did the cows talk too?"

"Moo! You're scaring the poor bird."

Eddy started to giggle, and Grandpa smiled.

"What happened next?" Eddy asked when he stopped laughing.

"Windham and I stood by quietly and watched. I felt sad and helpless, as the goose struggled in the water. He was very frightened, and splashed like crazy so he wouldn't drown. His sudden landing in the stream certainly caused excitement around the whole farm."

"Suddenly a new look of terror came over the goose. He stared at the different animals as they stood watching him. Our farm was a strange place for him and he wasn't alone!"

Chapter Six

FRIEND OR FOE

"The new visitor to the farm was a Canada Goose. I named him Max. He looked all around to see where he had landed. Max didn't know that he was on our farm. This lonely goose was lost and without his family. Somehow he had strayed away from his flock of geese. Maybe he couldn't fly fast enough. But his parents should have been with him."

"I saw Max gaze upwards. He was probably looking for his family. A few clouds floated across the blue sky, but no geese were in sight."

"Still in the water, Max looked at the many faces in front of him. They were all strangers! But he didn't know if they were friend or foe. The animals would help Max, but they frightened him with all of their unfamiliar noises. He probably thought he was in danger."

"Did Max escape?"

"He slowly stopped splashing, and the water became still and peaceful. Then suddenly, Max went into an attack mode. He looked and sounded dangerous with a loud hissing noise and his neck stretched out. The other animals were startled and scared, so many of them ran away from the riverbank. This made it possible for Max to escape."

"It was amazing! I watched Max rise up from the water and fly away. But his wings were still wet, so he didn't fly too fast. When he flew by, I noticed that he had a third deformed leg. It probably caused him to fly more slowly, so he couldn't keep up with his flock. That's why he landed here."

"Through the air, I followed him to see where he flew. As I watched him land, it looked like he was still on our farm. Out of the corner of my eye, I saw Windham run in the same direction that Max went. The young pig was already ahead of me. We both searched for Max."

"Did you find him?"

"Yes, we found Max in another area of our farm! But he stood in some tall grass in one of the pastures, so I didn't see him right away. He was shorter than most of the grass around him."

"Was Windham with you?"

"He was there, but not too close to me. His eyes were fixed on Max. We both watched as Max put his tiny feathers in place with a flutter. We heard him call with a frightened cry, as he looked upwards towards the sky."

"Where was his family? They would be looking for him."

"His parents were probably worried, but I didn't see any other geese. For a few minutes, the three of us stood still and stayed quiet. I've seen many Canada Geese before, but there was something special about Max. He didn't know that our farm was a friendly home. It was a new and strange place for him. He was probably very scared."

"Did Windham do anything to help?"

"He kept watch and didn't move. We both waited. Neither one of us wanted to leave."

Chapter Seven

BEST FRIENDS

"Max was the first one to move. He must have been hungry, because he started to eat some grass. I quietly took a few steps closer."

"I swat at an ugly black bug, and it flew away towards Max. Accidentally I sent it his way. But he probably enjoyed it. One second the bug was in front of Max, and the next moment it was in his mouth."

"He eats bugs? Ugh!"

"Max eats them for lunch, just like you have hotdogs."

Eddy laughed.

"I looked over at the field, where my dad drove his large tractor. A thunderous banging noise came from the machine. When I glanced back at Max, his whole body shook. The noise must have scared him."

"Suddenly, Max started to run. He moved quickly towards the area with shorter grass, where we stood. But he couldn't stop in time."

"Did Max see you?"

"He should have seen Windham in front of him. But it was too late! Max crashed right into the young pig. The two animals flew through the air and fell with a thud onto the ground."

"The pig flew too? We're they hurt?"

"I don't think so. Both animals stood and looked at each other. The goose took a step back without moving his eyes. Max looked so frightened! But Windham really surprised me. In the field, there were some colorful wildflowers, and Windham picked a few of them. He gave them to Max! That's how they first met."

"They were friends now?"

"From that day on, Windham and Max were best friends and always together."

"Wow!"

"They were quite the pair. But right now Eddy, we should go back to the house. I'll continue my story another day."

After saying goodnight to Peanut, Eddy and Grandpa slowly walked up the path towards the house. They arrived just in time for supper.

The earlier discussion about moving was not mentioned that night. Instead, Grandpa told some funny stories, and everyone laughed. When his bedtime arrived, Eddy wasn't a happy boy. But his mood changed when he was reminded that Grandpa would still be there in the morning.

- Chapter Eight -

FRIENDS & FAMILY

The next day after school, Eddy followed his usual schedule and visited some of the farm animals. But there was one big difference! His Grandpa joined him for some of his visits in the barns. Together they looked for Peanut, and found him alone again in the corner.

"I want to hear more of your story Grandpa," Eddy asked after they sat down with Peanut.

"I watched those two unusual friends and they amazed me. What a pair! This twosome was a pink pig, who enjoyed playing in the mud and a black headed goose that spent hours cleaning his feathers."

"That's funny. What games did they play together?"

"I saw them run and chase each other, like they played some sort of a game. Max would spread his wings to gain speed, and run past Windham. Every day, I saw them walk around the farm. They never went too close to the cows, but they visited all of the other animals. A lot of time was spent with the ducks, and they ate some of their corn."

"Are Max and the ducks cousins?"

"I think you're right Eddy."

"He missed his family."

"I'm sure he did. Sometimes I saw Max sit quietly alone with his long neck stretched upwards to the sky."

"Maybe he was praying."

"Yes, to find his family. One day, a flock of Canada Geese flew over us. Along with Max and Windham, I looked up at the group in their large V formation."

"Windham would be sad, if Max went away."

"Despite their differences, Max and Windham shared a warm friendship. They grew up together and formed a lifelong bond. Max did join a flock of geese after many years, but he always returned to visit Windham. Over the years, this farm couldn't imagine such an odd match of companions. I don't know if we'll see this happen again."

- Chapter Nine -

DAD'S LITTLE HELPER

On the following day, Eddy was alone for his visit to Peanut. He gently picked up the tiny piglet, as he sat alone in the corner of the pen.

"You're too young to be over here on your own!" Eddy exclaimed when he saw Peanut away from the warm lamps again.

Then Eddy had an idea! As he lifted the piglet up in his arms, Peanut let out a noisy squeal. But the noise did not discourage Eddy. This would help Peanut. He knew what this young animal needed.

When Eddy arrived at the next barn, he gently set the piglet down upon the straw covered floor. The blanket of straw was large enough to hold another small animal. Eddy was certain that Peanut would keep warm if he sat on the straw and stayed close to the other animals. He remained in the barn until his young piglet was comfortable. Eddy was happy! This was his best idea yet! His favourite piglet was no longer alone!

Eddy told Grandpa that he moved Peanut to the other barn. He agreed with his grandson that it was a great idea. Once again, the farm had another unusual pair of animals.

It was announced Friday night that a group of boy scouts were scheduled to tour the farm on Saturday afternoon. This was the first farm tour of the year. Unfortunately, Eddy was too young to help his dad with the tours.

Eddy was very sad when Grandpa left that night to go home. But he promised his grandson to talk with his dad about staying on the farm.

On Saturday afternoon, Eddy saw an unfamiliar boy standing alone by the duck pond. The boy's identity and his reason for being there, was a mystery. Eddy looked closely at the boy. He didn't wear farm clothes, and appeared to be a few years older than him. By the boy's brown shirt and shorts, Eddy wondered if this visitor was a boy scout.

"Are you a boy scout?"

"Yes," the boy answered shyly.

"Why are you standing here by yourself?" Eddy asked curiously.

"My name is Tommy." There was a noticeable stutter in his voice. "I came on the farm tour with the boy scouts, but I went on my own for a little walk. I'm different from the other scouts, and don't always feel like part of their group. I can't help it, but I stutter. You must hear it!"

"Do the boys tease you, or say anything to upset you?"

"No. But I'm new here, and trying to fit in. The way I talk makes it hard."

This gave Eddy another idea.

"Come with me Tommy. I want to show you something. You'll like it."

Eddy held Tommy's hand, and they walked towards one of the barns. Inside the barn, Tommy was surprised when he looked at the animals in front of him. He walked closer to see more clearly.

"Why is that little pig in here with all of these rabbits?" Tommy asked.

"I named him Peanut. He's here because the other pigs always ignored him. His long ears make him look different. With those ears, I put him with the rabbits. Their fur helps Peanut keep warm, and they all get along great!"

The rabbits accepted the young piglet into their group, and Peanut never wandered off on his own again.

That day on the farm changed both Eddy and Tommy! The two boys became friends, and Tommy was no longer shy when he met other children. He didn't worry anymore about fitting in. Seeing how the young piglet and some rabbits lived happily together gave him the courage that he needed. They were two totally different animals, but it did not matter.

A week later, another announcement was made at the dinner table. It was great news! Eddy and his family were staying at the farm!

"We're not moving?"

"No way! We're staying here on the farm, with all of the animals."

"Does Grandpa know?"

"Yes, I phoned and told him before supper."

"We're happy again!"

About once a month, different groups visited the farm, but there was one big exciting change.

"Welcome to our farm! I'm Eddy, my dad's little helper. He calls me his junior farm guide," he announces.

The huge smile on Eddy's face showed the happiness he felt inside. It was pleasure to help his dad with the farm tours. He was proud to show Peanut off to the crowds. Farmer John changed his mind about his son being too young for the tours. Eddy earned the new title when he helped the shy Boy Scout.

"Several animals know this farm as their home. What are some of the different animals our visitors will see today Eddy?" Farmer John asked.

"We have black and white cows, noisy chickens, ducks, rabbits, pigs, horses, and woolly lambs. My favourite animals are the pigs and rabbits. A litter of pigs is called a farrow. My dad put heat lamps in the barns to keep them warm. You will see my new pet, the star of the tour. His name is Peanut, the lop-eared piglet."

The tour ended at the small red barn that housed the young piglet. A bright pink star and the name Peanut were painted above the barn door. The visitors walked inside to view the farm celebrity, and everyone was surprised by the animals. Peanut amazed all of the children and adults, as he fit in perfectly with the rabbits. News of the lop-eared piglet spread fast. Peanut was one special pig!

Chartered buses travelled many miles to see the famous pig at the family farm. To direct the large number of visitors, Farmer John put up a new sign for the farm tours. Eddy was delighted and excited to tell the story about Peanut and the rabbits. After all, it was his idea! The farm was home to another special and unusual pair of companions!

CPSIA information can be obtained
at www.ICGtesting.com
Printed in the USA
LVIC04n0007010414
379705LV00001B/1